aR 2.4

W9-CQS-564

E
WAB   Waber, Bernard

           But names will
           never hurt me

DATE DUE $13.95

by BERNARD WABER

But Names
Will Never Hurt Me

Houghton Mifflin Company, Boston

for ETHEL

Library of Congress Cataloging in Publication Data

Waber, Bernard.
 But names will never hurt me.

 SUMMARY: How Alison Wonderland got her name and how
she learned to live with it.
 [1. Names, Personal — Fiction] I. Title.
PZ7.W113Bu   [E]   75-40473
ISBN 0-395-24383-1

Printed in the United States of America
H   10   9   8   7   6   5

Alison.
Alison Wonderland.
Your name.

It began with your grandparents, Alison.
Their name: Voonterlant.
Heloise and Fredrich Voonterlant.
When they got off the boat,
the boat that brought them to these shores,
the man at the gate,
the man who checked all of their papers,
couldn't, for some reason, pronounce Voonterlant.
If he had tried, perhaps he could have.

But he was busy, this man—very busy.
Hundreds of people were passing through the gate.
So he wrote on their papers a name he could
spell and pronounce: Wonderland.
In minutes, your grandparents became
Heloise and Fredrich Wonderland.

"This is a new land—a new beginning.
  We are happy to be here.
  Let it be Wonderland,"
  said your grandmother.
"No problem," said your grandfather.

And so, Alison,
your grandparents settled in the new land.
They were happy.
In time, a son was born to them—your father.
"Let's call him Daniel," said your grandmother.
"No problem," said your grandfather.

7

Your father grew up
and married.

In time, your mother was pregnant—
with you Alison, only she didn't know
for certain it was going to be you.

"If it's a boy,
let's name him
William,"
said your mother.
"No problem,"
said your father.

"Now, let's think of a girl's name,"
 said your mother.
"How about Caroline?" said your father.
"How about Deborah?" said your mother.
"How about Lisa?" said your father.
"How about Wendy?" said your mother.

"Do you want to know something?" said your
mother. "There's a girl's name I have
always loved."
"What is it?" asked your father.
"Alison," said your mother.
Your father thought about it.
"Alison. Alison Wonderland.
That's a problem," said your father.
"You mean . . . It sounds too much like . . ."
"Yes," said your father.

"How about Jennifer?" said your father.
"How about Kim?" said your mother.
"How about Denise?" said your father.

"Do you want to know something?"
said your mother.
"What?" said your father.
"I still love the name Alison."
Your father thought about it.
"Alison. Alison Wonderland.
It's still a problem," said your father.
"I know," said your mother.

In January, your father said,
"How about Joanne?"

In February, your mother said,
"How about Nancy?"

In March, your father said,
"How about Dianne?"

In April, your mother said,
"How about Judy?"

In May, your father said,
"How about if we decide already."

14

In June, your mother said,
"Do you want to know something?
I still love the name Alison."
"Do you want to know something else?"
said your father. "I'm beginning to
get used to it. Maybe it's not
such a problem."
"Maybe not," said your mother.

In July, your mother said, "Let's.
If it's a girl, let's name her Alison."
"No problem," said your father.

In August, you were born.
And you were named Alison.
Alison Wonderland.
"What a beautiful baby!"
said your grandmother.
"What a beautiful name!"
said your grandfather.
And there were no problems.

Yours was a happy babyhood, Alison.

But it wasn't long before you began
having problems.
Your family moved to a new neighborhood—
a new school.
The teacher called roll:
"Tod Brown!" — "Here!"
"George Falco!" — "Here!"
"Lucy Gomez!" — "Here!"
"Stacey Klinghoffer!" — "Here!"
"Jason Segal!" — "Here!"
"Joseph Sheehan!" — "Here!"
"Holly Williams!" — "Here!"
"Alison Wonderland!" —

ALISON WONDERLAND!!!
Everyone, everyone in the entire class
turned around and stared at you in
astonishment, Alison.
You didn't even have to answer "Here!"
Your unhappy face spoke for you.

But that was just the beginning, Alison.
There was that day, for example,
during soft-ball practice.
You were reaching for a high fly,
when some kid, some really smart-alecky kid,
yelled out,
"Hey, Alison Wonderland,
watch out for rabbit holes!"

Of course,
you fumbled the ball.

And there was another day,
a really rotten day.
You came across this envelope
on your school desk.
It was pretty, pastel yellow.
You opened it eagerly, hoping it was
an invitation to a party.
It was a party invitation, all right —
and it read:

Dear Alison Wonderland,

> You are invited to a party —
> a tea party.
> Please be prompt.
>
>> Signed,
>> The Mad Hatter

You crumpled the letter and were
immediately sorry.
Everyone was watching.

And how will you forget the day
"Gootch" Simpson got you at a bad moment,
when he called out for at least
the hundredth time,
"Hey Alison! Alison Wonderland!
Seen any white rabbits lately? Ha, ha, ha!"
And then he went into his stupid
little song and dance:
"It's late! It's late!
Dum-ditty, dum-ditty,
Dum-dum-dum!"

Well, you leaped at him,
wrestled him to the ground, and held him
down until he apologized.
But that didn't make you feel better.

27

You burst into the house with tears.

"Why!" you cried out to your mother.

"Why, with thousands of names to choose from,
did you have to go and pick a name like Alison?
Alison Wonderland! A joke!"

Your mother held you and tried to comfort you.
And then she said,
"It may have been wrong,
It may very well have been wrong.
But, Alison, this was a name given to you
with, oh, so much love.
If you just remember that,
nothing, no remark,
will ever hurt you again."

That was good advice.
I should know.
Because
you grew up
to be me.

ANIMAL
HOSPITAL

DR. ALISON WONDERLAND
Veterinarian

"Dr. Wonderland,
 my rabbit is sick.
 Can you make him better?"

"Well, come right in.
 And don't worry.
 I know all about rabbits."